TOUCHLINE TERROR!

AND OTHER STORIES:

GRUESOME GOALKEEPING
DIRTY DEFENDING

MICHAEL COLEMAN
ILLUSTRATED BY NICK ABADZIS

ORCHARD BOOKS

Look out for the other Angels FC books:

SHOCKING SHOOTING
DAZZLING DRIBBLING
SQUABBLING SQUADS
AWESOME ATTACKING

ORCHARD BOOKS
338 Euston Road, London NW1 3BH
Orchard Books Australia
Level 17/205 Kent St, Sydney, NSW 2000

First published in Great Britain as individual volumes
First published in Great Britain in this bind-up format 2004
This edition published 2008
Touchline Terror
Text © Michael Coleman 1997, inside illustrations © Nick Abadzis 1997
Gruesome Goalkeeping
Text © Michael Coleman 1997, inside illustrations © Nick Abadzis 1997
Dirty Defending
Text © Michael Coleman 1997, inside illustations © Nick Abadzis 1997

The rights of Michael Coleman to be identified as the author
and of Nick Abadzis to be identified as the illustrator of this work
have been asserted by them in accordance with the
Copyright, Designs and Patents Act, 1988.
A CIP catalogue record for this book is available
from the British Library.

ISBN 978 1 40830 014 5

1 3 5 7 9 10 8 6 4 2
Printed in Great Britain by
CPI Cox & Wyman, Reading, RG1 8EX

Orchard Books is a division of Hachette Children's Books
an Hachette Livre UK company.
www.hachettelivre.co.uk

A HILARIOUS HAT TRICK OF STORIES!

To all the football fans (and non-football fans)
at St Peter's Catholic Primary School,
Waterlooville
M.C.

For Lola
N.A.

TOUCHLINE
TERROR

CONTENTS

1

The Game of the Century

"Get stuck in, Colin!"

"Get back, Colin!"

"Get forward, Colin!"

"Keep going, Colin!"

"Good tackle, Colin!"

"Go on, Colin!"

"Shoot!"

"Goal!! Yes!! Goalie-goalie-GOOAAALLLL!!"

"Well played, Colin! Well played, Angels!"

Colin "Colly" Flower, the Angels FC striker, trotted across to the car that was waiting for him. He slid into the passenger seat.

"Well played, son," croaked the man at the wheel. He sounded as if he'd been shouting a lot.

"Thanks, Dad," said Colly.

"Yep, you played well today. Really well."

The car moved off and Colly tucked his sports bag between his feet. Wait for it, wait for it, he thought. Any minute now.

11

"Oh, yes," repeated Mr Flower.
"Really well."

A gap appeared in the stream of traffic passing along the road outside the park gates. Colly's dad swung the car out and accelerated. Here it comes, thought Colly: "Except for…"

"Except for…"

His heart sank. It was always the same after a match. He would get into the car. His dad would tell him how well he'd played. But then, inside a minute, he'd be saying the two words that made Colly feel as though he wanted to put his head under a heavy blanket. (His own head or his dad's, it didn't much matter which.)

Colly decided to get it over and done with quickly.

"Except for what?" he said.

"Except for," said Colly's dad, "that time you lost the ball in the centre circle."

"Lost the ball? When?"

"In the thirty-eighth minute, it was. I checked my watch. Their midfielder tackled you just as you were turning."

"That was the only tackle I lost all game, Dad!"

"True, true. But it put them on the attack. They could have scored." Mr Flower glanced Colly's way. "That's it, son. Just thought I'd mention it."

Colly waited. "Well…and then there was…" usually came next.

"Well…and then there was that free kick of yours that scraped the bar. I thought you should really have scored there."

"I scored two afterwards, didn't I?" said Colly irritably.

"True, true. Good 'uns they were too. But if you'd banged in that free kick instead of scraping the bar – well, you'd have ended up with a hat trick, wouldn't you? Now, I was watching you closely. You leaned back just a fraction as you hit it. Result – you got your foot under it, see? You need to be over the ball. Get that head down, son."

"Nothing else, then?" asked Colly between gritted teeth.

"Nope. Not a thing."

Colly saw that they'd just turned into their road. That could only mean "Apart from…"

"Apart from…" began Mr Flower.

"What? What? Apart from what?" squawked Colly, his temperature rising.

"That sloppy pass."

"What sloppy pass? I didn't make a sloppy pass from start to finish!"

"Yes, you did."

"When? When?" shouted Colly.

"During the kick-in before the game. When you, Rhoda O'Neill and Lionel Murgatroyd were passing it in a triangle. You went to chip it to Rhoda and hit it too hard and low. She had to run and get it back from that dog. Remember?"

Colly sighed. "I remember."

It was then, as Mr Flower burbled on about relaxing into chipped passes, that Colly came to his decision. He loved having his dad watch him. Rain or shine, hard frost or howling gale, he was always there, the most enthusiastic supporter on the touchline. But these inquests on the way home were driving him bonkers. His dad was turning into a real touchline terror! Somehow, Colly had decided, he had to make him stop. But how?

⚽   ⚽   ⚽

"Right, everybody, listen in. This is your chance to have your say about a significant world event." Everybody looked towards the man standing at the front of the room.

"What sort of significant world event, Trev?" said Lennie Gould loudly. "Picking the next England team?"

"Striker, Colly Flower!" called Kirsten Browne, the Angels goalkeeper.

Laughing, Trevor Rowe held up a hand
for order. "No, not that. Mind you, if they
ever do ask me to leave the Angels and
coach the England team, I might well take
up your suggestion, Kirsten!"

Everybody smiled. It was rumoured that
Trev could have been good enough to play
football for England, if he hadn't wanted to
be a vicar more. Because that's what he was.

The team were all members of the St Jude's Youth Club and Trev, besides being the Angels coach, was vicar of St Jude's Church. That was one reason why Colly's team were called Angels FC. The other was that Trev insisted on fair play. "Angels on and off the pitch!" was his motto and the team weren't allowed to forget it. Which made the wicked idea that Colly was about to have all the more surprising…

"No," continued Trev, "the significant world event I'm referring to is the fact that this is St Jude's centenary year – it's one hundred years since the church was built. So I'm planning a whole series of special events. And that's where you lot come in. Any ideas for something involving the Angels?"

Everybody fell silent for a moment as they thought.

Then Bazza Watts called out, "How about a football exhibition?"

Daisy Higgins, the team's centre-back, wasn't impressed. "What – round footballs, square footballs, oblong footballs, footballs with holes in the middle—"

"You'll have a hole in your middle if you don't watch it," growled Bazza. "I mean an exhibition of things to do with football. We could write to famous people. Get them to donate something. An old football shirt or an old pair of boots…"

"My dad's got an old pair
of boots," said Lulu
Squibb.

"Has he?"

"Concrete ones."
She laughed. "He
grows flowers in them."

It must have been the mention of flowers
and dads that did it, thought Colly
afterwards. Whatever the reason, that's
when his devilish idea arrived, whistling
into his head like a well-struck shot.

"How about a players versus parents
football match!" he yelled.

The moment he heard the suggestion, Trev's eyes lit up. "Colly – that's a brilliant idea!" He began scribbling furiously. "We could call it 'The Game of the Century'. We could produce a programme. And I'll write officially to the parents, inviting them to put their names forward…"

He stopped and sucked the end of his pen. "Hmm, what about the parents, though? Will enough of them agree to play?"

Colly spoke up straight away. His dad was going to discover that out there in the middle, football was a tough game!

"My dad'll play, Trev. You can put him down top of your list. Number one! Flower, Henry Montgomery. A definite!"

2

Second Thoughts

Colly spent the next couple of days hugging himself with pleasure. What a brilliant idea! It was all he could do to keep quiet about it. He just couldn't wait for Trev's letter to arrive, inviting his dad to play in "The Game of the Century".

And then Wednesday came. During the football season, Wednesday evenings meant Training Over the Park with Dad.

"Let's start with tackling," said Colly's dad. "A good tackle has all your weight going in behind it, son. You lost that one on Saturday because you were off balance. Look, let me show you. I've studied all the best players on the telly, so I know just how to do it."

Mr Flower put the ball on the ground between himself and Colly. "Block tackle, OK?" He demonstrated in slow motion. "Use the side of your foot and leeeeean into it. Right, now try to tackle me."

"You sure?" said Colly.

"Come on, come on. I won't hurt you."

"OK." Colly sighed.

As his dad moved forward to the ball, Colly surged in. Thundering through with his right foot, he hit his dad with one of his best tackles. The effect was dramatic. Mr Flower's right leg was jerked back, his left foot slid to one side – and the rest of him went up into the air.

"Yes...well," said Mr Flower as he picked himself up, "good. You're learning, son. If you'd done that on Saturday, you'd have been all right. Now then. Free kicks."

Again, Colly's dad placed the ball on the ground, this time with Colly being sent off to stand between the goalposts. "Point the toe…" Mr Flower demonstrated, looking like a tubby ballet dancer.

Placing the ball on the edge of the penalty area, Colly's dad took five slow paces backwards. Then he ran in, commentating as he went.

"Lean forward. Point toe. Go through the ball. Ooops!"

Colly gazed after the ball as it shot off at a right angle, curving wildly as it flew across the path at the side of the pitch and ploughed into an ornamental pond.

"Did you see how I got that shot to bend in the air?" said Mr Flower as they fished the ball out. "Easy when you know how. Inside of the foot, cutting sharply across the surface of the ball to impart maximum spin."

"I thought you were showing me how to keep the ball down?" said Colly.

"It did stay down, didn't it?"

"Yeah," muttered Colly. "Like a submarine."

As they trudged back to the grass, Colly's heart was sinking like a submarine too. What had he done? Getting his own back by suggesting a parents versus players match had seemed a good idea at the time, but now he wasn't so sure. Come the match, everybody was going to see how useless his dad was at football. And that meant the embarrassment was going to be total.

"Right, son," Mr Flower was saying. "Chipped passes. The secret here is to reeeelaxxxxxxxx…"

But Colly wasn't listening. He'd just made another decision: Henry Montgomery Flower was definitely not going to play in "The Game of the Century"!

The question this time was: how could Colly stop him?

3

Hitting the Post

Colly lay in bed thinking the problem over. It was tricky. His dad was bound to want to play when he got Trev's invitation. So, was there anything he could say that would persuade Trev not to send one? Not a chance. Colly had been too convincing. So if the invitation was definitely coming, what he had to do was think of some rock-solid reasons why Mr Flower shouldn't accept it once it arrived. Assuming it did arrive, of course.

29

Colly punched his pillow in delight. That was it! His dad couldn't accept an invitation that never arrived, could he? So, how could he get to that letter first? That would be the tricky bit.

Ever since their nutty dog, Gnawman, had shown itself to be particularly partial to a breakfast of anything that plopped through their letter box, Mr Flower had taken to waiting by the door until the post arrived.

There was only one solution, realised Colly. He was going to have to get up early enough to intercept the invitation before it reached the door. Yes, for the first time in his footballing life he had to make sure he hit the post!

⚽   ⚽   ⚽

They were into the last minute in the Cup Final. After being 2–0 down against Manchester United, a brilliant Colly hat trick had put the Angels 3–2 ahead. All they had to do was play out time. Winning the ball with another perfectly timed tackle, Colly dribbled it lazily towards the corner flag. Hold on to it, he told himself. There can't be long to go. The crowd are whistling...whistling...

Whistling!

Leaving his dream, Colly shot up in bed. He'd overslept! The postwoman was on the other side of the road, whistling cheerfully as usual. Any minute now she'd be at their door, shoving Trev's invitation into his dad's waiting hands!

Diving out of bed, Colly snatched up his trousers – and threw them down again. No time! If he was going to intercept that letter before it reached their door he was going to have to go just as he was. In his West Ham pyjamas!

Scuttling down the stairs, Colly dived out of the back door and round the side of the house. He was in the nick of time. The postwoman had just reached their front gate as he raced out to meet her.

"Morning, morning," said Colly brightly. "Anything for us?"

The postwoman looked down at Colly's claret and blue pyjamas. "There might be," she said. "Why, what are we expecting? Dressing gown? A pair of fluffy slip-slops?"

Colly gave her the sort of glare he usually reserved for defenders who kicked him. "Letters," he growled. "Just letters."

The postwoman handed over a pile of envelopes. Colly quickly sorted through them. There it was! A long brown envelope with a picture of St Jude's Church on the front and their address in Trev's neat handwriting.

Colly shoved it inside his pyjama jacket. Then, keeping it in place by holding an arm across his waist, he padded up the garden path. All he had to do now was put the rest of the post through the letter box and—

"Colin? What are you doing?"

As his dad swung open the front door, Colly stopped dead. This wasn't supposed to happen! His dad must have heard the postwoman go by and wondered why she hadn't left anything. Now what was he going to do?

"Er…"

"And why are you in the front garden in your pyjamas?" continued Mr Flower.

Pyjamas! thought Colly. I'm still in my pyjamas! Maybe if I pretend I am sleepwalking…

Slowly, Colly raised his arms and closed his eyes until they were the narrowest of slits. Then he began to totter stiff-legged up the path.

"Post for Mr Flower," he said, talking like a robot. "Post for Mr Flower."

"Colin? Are you all right?"

"Special delivery," said Colin, flicking his eyes open and then closing them again.

Mr Flower frowned. "Overnight delivery by the look of it," he said, staring at Colly's pyjamas. "Are you sleepwalking, son?"

"Yes," said Colly, without stopping. Past his astonished dad he went, up the stairs and into his bedroom. He'd done it!

Now to destroy that letter. Fishing inside his pyjama jacket, Colly felt for the long brown envelope. It had gone! He ripped open the buttons and looked again. Skin! Nothing but skin! It must have fallen out while I was pretending to sleepwalk, he thought. But in that case, where is it? A sudden shout from downstairs told him exactly where.

"Hey! Colin! Hey!"

Colly flung open his door. There, at the bottom of the stairs, was his dad. And in his hand was Trev's letter.

"There's going to be a parents against players match!" cried Mr Flower. "Trev wants to know if I'll play."

"And will you?" asked Colly.

Mr Flower shook his head slowly. "Oh, Colin. I'm not going to—"

"Not going to?" yelled Colly, his hopes soaring. "Did you say you're not going to play?"

"And upset you, son?" said Mr Flower. "Never! What I was about to say was: I'm not going to miss this for anything!"

A Ripping Time

As the days went by, Colly lived in hope that his dad would change his mind. But, if anything, he got more and more enthusiastic about it. Nothing Colly could say would put him off.

"Kirsten reckons the parents' team are going to get smashed," said Colly at breakfast two days before the game.

"Oh, yes?" said Mr Flower.

"Pulverised, Lennie Gould reckons," added Colly. "Tarlock reckons you're going to get trounced, Daisy reckons you're going to get dumped, Mick reckons you're in for a mangling, Lulu says it'll be a lashing, Rhoda thinks you're in for a real roasting and both Jeremy and Jonjo think it'll be a joy-ride for us."

"Hmm," said Mr Flower. "How about Bazza Watts?"

"He reckons you're going to get whipped, walloped and whacked," said Colly. "He's bet Lennie that he can kick every parent who's playing."

"Really?" Colly's dad merely smiled. "I think Mrs Watts will have something to say about that. She's playing right wing for us."

"Mrs Watts is playing? You're kidding!"

"No, I'm not. She used to be an international hockey player. And she's not a bad footballer by all accounts. If there's any whipping, walloping and whacking to be done, I bet she'll be the one who's doing it!"

Colly closed his eyes in despair. Not only was his dad going to be shown up by the other dads – he was even going to be shown up by one of the mums as well! Mrs Watts would still be running when his dad was on his knees.

In desperation, Colly had one last idea. If he couldn't stop his dad wanting to play, could he arrange things so that he wouldn't be able to play because he was simply too tired..?

"Dad! I'm worried about you," said Colly, putting on what he hoped was a worried look. "Are you sure you're fit enough for this game?"

"Fit? Me?" said Mr Flower. "Ridiculous question! Of course I am."

Colly grinned. "Then you won't mind coming on a little training run with me, will you?"

"Er...no. When?"

"How about tomorrow evening?"

They set off straight after tea. Colly led the way. "How far do you want to go?" called Mr Flower. "Not far," called Colly over his shoulder. "Down to the park, round the boating lake a couple of times, along the towpath by the canal, up to the lock gates and back home through town. Can't be more than ten kilometres. OK?"

"Er…fine," said Mr Flower, already panting for breath. "Fine…"

They got as far as the park – almost. Gasping for breath, Mr Flower collapsed on to the bench just outside the park gates.

43

"You all right, Dad?" said Colly as he helped his dad home again.

"Course...gasp...I am...gasp...son... gasp," gasped Mr Flower.

"You don't sound it," said Colly as his dad opened the front door. "And you don't look it," he added as Mr Flower immediately flopped down on to the hall carpet.

"Never...judge...by appearances," gasped Mr Flower, his mouth opening and closing like a fish out of water. "A match...is different."

"It is?" said Colly.

"Oh, yes." Mr Flower tapped the side of his head. "You use your head, son. Let the ball do the work…"

"Dad! The game's tomorrow!" Colly shook his head in despair. "You can't still want to play?"

"Of course I do!" said Colly's dad, finding enough energy to sit up. "Why do you think I've bought that lot?" He pointed to a brand-new sports bag, sitting in the corner of the hallway.

"What lot?" asked Colly.

"New football gear, of course! Shirt, shorts, socks – even a new pair of boots. Colin, you won't recognise me when I step on to that pitch!"

This is it, thought Colly. The end. The absolute end. With brand new gear, his dad was going to look so good that everyone would expect him to play like a wizard. Then they'd learn the truth! Oh, the embarrassment!

⚽ ⚽ ⚽

As he walked downstairs early the next morning, Colly's spirits couldn't have been lower if the Angels had been bottom of the league with no hope of escaping relegation.

Gloomily he opened the kitchen door, only to be met by Gnawman pounding out to meet him, his tail going round like a windmill.

"Hello, boy. Nice to see you're happy at least."

The dog scampered out to the front door, then back again. Colly ruffled his fur.

"It's Sunday, dimbo. No post today. Nothing to chew…"

As the thought struck him, Colly's eyes settled on Mr Flower's new sports bag sitting on the hall stand.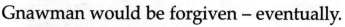

Could he? Should he? It was a desperate thing he was thinking of, he knew that. But he was desperate. And Gnawman would be forgiven – eventually.

Tiptoeing into the hall, Colly lifted his dad's bag. Gnawman followed him to the front door, panting excitedly.

"Sssh!" Colly said to the dog. "You wait there. You're going to enjoy this."

Opening the front door, Colly stepped outside. He unzipped his dad's sports bag. And then, piece by piece, he began to feed Mr Flower's brand-new football gear back in through the letter box.

His new shirt disappeared in a trice, wrenched from Colly's hand as Gnawman tugged it through. Moments later, Colly heard sounds of ripping.

Colly managed to get one of the new football boots through the letter box next, which Gnawman leapt on as if it were a cat. This was followed by his dad's new socks and finally, his new shorts.

Colly waited for a couple of minutes, then opened the front door. The sight that greeted him was even better than he'd hoped for. Scraps of material were everywhere, with not a thing left that was wearable. In the middle of it all, still chewing happily on the remains of Mr Flower's right boot, sat Gnawman.

Beautiful! With joy in his heart, Colly dashed up to his room to start getting his own football gear together.

Now he really could enjoy "The Game of the Century"!

5

Number One

"You mean your dad's not playing after all, Colly?" said Kirsten, pulling on her goalkeeper's gloves.

Colly shook his head. He tried to look sad. "Afraid not. Bit of an accident in the home, dog-wise."

"That's no good," moaned Bazza Watts. "How am I going to kick my full set of parents now? Your dad should be ashamed of himself."

Not as ashamed as I'd have been of him, thought Colly. He smiled as he remembered what his dad had been doing when he left for the game – holding the tatters of his new gear and muttering to himself about dogs' homes and insurance policies.

"Maybe you can kick him while he's on the touchline, Bazza," laughed Lulu Squibb.

Tarlock Bhasin turned to Colly. "He will be watching as usual, won't he?"

"I reckon so," said Colly as they left the changing room with a clattering of studs. He sighed loudly. "It's such a pity, though. I really wanted my dad to play in this match…"

"I know you did, son," came a familiar voice. "And I wasn't going to let you down. So here I am!"

Colly stopped, open-mouthed. In front of him stood his dad – changed and ready to play!

From behind him he heard loud spluttering noises, like a collection of balloons going down. It was the rest of the Angels team, trying not to laugh.

"Like your gear, Mr Flower!" said Jonjo Rix.

"Yeah," laughed Rhoda O'Neill. "Where d'you get it – the museum?"

"No," replied Colly's dad, grinning. "Out of the attic. It's my old school kit. When Gnawman chewed up my new stuff it was all I had left."

Colly blinked. The sight was awful. It was pretty obvious that his dad had grown a lot since leaving school. Everything looked as if it was bursting at the seams. His shirt was tight across his chest and didn't quite reach down as far as his shorts. Or maybe it was his shorts that didn't quite reach his shirt – Colly couldn't tell. Even his dad's socks looked too small, bulging fit to burst with a huge pair of shinpads inside them so that they came only halfway up his legs.

And as for his boots…when Colly saw the cracked and battered things on his dad's feet, with his big toes clearly visible, he wished the centre circle would open up and swallow him whole.

"Hello, Mr Flower. I'm so glad you could play." It was Trev, referee's whistle round his neck.

Colly's dad did a quick sprint on the spot. "All systems go, Trev! Where do you want me? Centre forward, barnstorming through the middle? Out wide, ball-juggling my way down the touchline? What position?"

"What position?" echoed Trev. "In goal, of course."

In *goal*?!

"Well...yes," said Trev. "When Colly said at our meeting to put you down as number one, I naturally assumed you were a goalie. All the other positions are filled now."

"Oh," said Mr Flower. He shrugged. "Oh, well. Goal it is, then. I'll do my best."

In goal! Brilliant! Colly heaved a huge sigh of relief. As he watched his dad trundle across the pitch to stand between the posts, Colly realised that things had worked out after all. OK, so his dad would be hopeless in goal, but that didn't matter. He'd be able to use the excuse that he was playing out of position. And, smiled Colly, with a bit of luck his dad would soon be so muddy that his ancient football kit wouldn't show him up either!

Perfect, he thought as Trev whistled to start the match. Surely nothing could go wrong now. But it could. And it did. What went wrong was that Mr Flower didn't turn out to be hopeless in goal. Quite the opposite, in fact. He turned out to be sensational. Colly got his first inkling of just how sensational as Mick Ryall sprinted down the right wing and hit a low cross into the penalty area. Colly hit it on the run. Wallop! Straight towards the bottom corner.

"Goa— " he began to shout…until suddenly Mr Flower flung himself across the goal and tipped the ball round the post!

The applause had hardly died down when Mr Flower did it again. As the corner came over, the ball was nodded out to Colly, lurking on the edge of the area. He met it with one of his best headers, a full-blooded effort which was rocketing towards the top corner – until Mr Flower flung himself up and back to punch it clear.

From then on the match was virtually one-way traffic. Apart from Mrs Watts having a goal disallowed because she was sitting on Bazza as she scrambled the ball over the line, it was all Angels. Only Colly's dad, making one stupendous save after another, stood between them and a famous victory.

"Hey, your dad's good, isn't he?" said Lennie Gould as the whistle blew for half-time with the score still at 0–0.

"Yes," said Colly cheerfully. "Isn't he just!"

It was Jeremy Emery who pointed out the drawback. "I do believe that you're not going to score today, Colin!"

Colly frowned. Jeremy could be right – and that would be all wrong too. He didn't mind his dad having a good game, he was delighted in fact, but the last thing he wanted was for him to play so well that he, Colly, didn't score a goal. If that happened his reputation as the Angels top marksman was going to be seriously dented.

"There you're wrong, Jeremy," Colly said grimly. "He can't keep me out for ever."

But, as the second half wore on, it began to look more and more as if Mr Flower could do just that. Every effort Colly put in was saved. His dad dashed out to dive at his feet when he was put through. He swooped like an eagle to stop his shots. On one occasion he even caught one of Colly's fiercest thunderbolts with one hand!

"Come on, Colly!" yelled Daisy Higgins from the back four. "Call yourself a striker?"

Still 0–0 and no more than a couple of minutes to go, thought Colly. It's got to be now or never.

Suddenly he saw his chance. As his striking partner Jonjo Rix picked the ball up in midfield, the parents' wheezing and spluttering defence opened up.

"Jonjo!"

Colly set off, timing his run perfectly to meet Jonjo's through ball. He looked up. His dad was rushing to meet him, plonking his battered boots down as he ran. Colly didn't hesitate. As his dad got close, Colly feinted to go one way and then darted the other – only to be pulled down by a hand stretching out and whipping his legs from under him.

PEEEEP!

"Penalty!" Trev was pointing to the spot.

"It was an accident, Trev," said Mr Flower. "I went for the ball!"

"Come on, Trev," said Mrs Watts, laughing. "Forgive him his trespasses."

"I have forgiven him," said Trev, trying to look serious. "He should have had a red card. But it's still a penalty."

Lennie Gould, the Angels penalty-taker, strode forward and carefully placed the ball on the spot. As Mr Flower went back to crouch on his goal line, Colly didn't know what to think. He was happy now.

His reputation was intact. If he hadn't been
fouled he'd have scored, no doubt about it.
So now what he wanted was for the team to
win. Or did he? No, he realised, he didn't.
What he wanted most of all was for the
Flower family to have a double triumph.
He wanted his dad to save this
penalty and keep a
clean sheet!

And he could help it happen! As Lennie paced carefully back, Colly pointed deliberately to the bottom corner of the goal, to his dad's right. It was where Lennie always hit his penalties.

Mr Flower nodded. Lennie ran in. He hit the shot, straight towards the bottom corner as usual…and Mr Flower dived headlong – the other way!

A 1–0 victory for the Angels! The players had beaten the parents!

"Well played, Dad," said Colly as his dad drove them home.

"Thanks, son," said Mr Flower.

Colly smiled. Thinking about things in the changing room, he'd decided that, after all, everything really had turned out excellently. He'd played a good game, winning the penalty. The Angels had won the match. And his dad had played a blinder.

Now there was only one thing left to do to make it a perfect day. The final part of his plan swung into action.

"Yep," said Colly, "you played well today, Dad. Really well."

"Thanks again, son."

"Except for…"

Mr Flower frowned. "Except for?"

Colly nodded. He'd taken the bait.
"Except for that penalty," he said seriously.

"What about that penalty?" said his dad.
"I didn't have a chance. Lennie Gould hit it perfectly."

"You went the wrong way," said Colly.
"I pointed to show you which way
it was going."

"Ah, but I thought he'd seen you point," said Mr Flower, raising his voice, "so I didn't know whether he'd hit it in his usual spot or change his mind and go for the other side!"

THEN YOU SHOULD HAVE **WATCHED THE BALL!**

WATCH THE BALL?

"Good goalkeepers don't watch the ball," shouted Mr Flower, "they watch the kicker so they can work out where he's going to place it!"

"But you didn't work it out, did you?" shouted Colly, even louder.

"Because he wiggled his knees!" bellowed
Mr Flower, now going red in the face.
"Anyway, what about all the good saves I
made!"

"What good saves?" yelled Colly.

"What good saves?" bawled Mr Flower.
"What do you mean, what good saves!!"

Bringing the car to a screeching halt, he
swung round – only to find Colly grinning
from ear to ear.

"Tell you what, Dad. I won't criticise you, if you won't criticise me. Agreed?"

A slow smile spread across Mr Flower's face as he saw the funny side. He put his hand out for Colly to shake. "Agreed!" he said and they both laughed.

GRUESOME
GOALKEEPING

CONTENTS

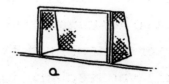

1

Butterfingers Browne!

Kirsten Browne, Angels FC's goalkeeper, knocked the drip off the end of her nose with the back of her glove.

Her hair looked like soggy spaghetti. Her football gear was dribbling more than the trickiest winger. The ground around her looked like a sea of brown jelly and, when she tried to lift her feet, sounded like it too. Squelch, squelch.

"Not much fun being a goalie, eh?" said a voice.

Kirsten risked a quick look round, although she knew exactly who had spoken. 'Cap Man,' was her name for him. He was a tall man, never without his flat cap and walking stick, who regularly stopped to watch the Angels matches.

"It is when you're winning a cup match!" replied Kirsten cheerfully.

And the Angels were winning, 1-0, against Harnett Rovers.

"Although it's more like a bucket match than a cup match," muttered Kirsten to herself as she turned back to the game.

The rain had been pouring down for the past two days and the pitch was in a dreadful state. Even the Angels goal, scored by their midfielder Micky Ryall, had been a bit of a fluke. His shot had been going wide when it had hit a large blob of mud and changed direction to whistle into the Harnett net. Kirsten shook her drenched hair like a dog sending spray everywhere. Still, there couldn't be more than a couple of minutes left. All they had to do was hang on to their lead and she'd soon be back in the warm, dry changing room celebrating their victory.

"Ginger's ball!"

Kirsten heard the sudden screech before she spotted the danger coming her way. Harnett's star player, a fiery ginger-headed boy with amazingly baggy shorts, had slipped the ball to a team-mate and was splashing through a gap in the Angels defence as he screamed for the return pass.

It came, the perfect one-two. Ginger was through, and racing her way!

"Go to meet him!" said the voice from behind her goal.

Kirsten splurged forward through the muddy goalmouth – then stopped. What was she doing? What did Cap Man know about goalkeeping? He didn't look as though he could tell one end of a football boot from the other.

Besides, the Angels right-back, Bazza Watts, was covering the move. Cap Man obviously hadn't seen him. So much for touchline experts! Kirsten stayed put, confident that Bazza had it all under control.

Unfortunately, Bazza didn't even have his own feet under control. Realising that he'd got his angle of approach all wrong, the Angels player tried to change direction. It was a disaster. Bazza's feet went one way but his body went the other. As the full-back dived into the mud like a hippopotamus on holiday, Ginger raced on into the penalty area.

This time, Kirsten did go to meet him.
She'd lost a valuable couple of seconds
though, and it made all the difference.
Instead of reaching Ginger in time to whip
the ball off his toe, she was a fraction late.
He got to it first and toe-poked the ball past
her – only to slip over himself! Desperately,
Kirsten swung round. A metre away, the
Harnett player was on the ground, sliding
head-first towards the ball in a mess of mud
and water. It was her chance! If she could
only dive and get that ball…

Kirsten launched herself towards it. Splosh! Mud shot up everywhere as she landed. But, even as she closed her eyes, Kirsten thrust her hands out – and grabbed the ball! She'd done it! The firm, round shape was in her hands!

What's more, the referee's whistle was shrieking for full-time. Or was it? The whistle had only gone *peep!* instead of the usual up-and-down *pee-ya-peep!* that signalled the end of a game. But what else could it be blowing for?

Even as she wondered, other confusing questions crowded into her mind. What was Ginger yelling about? And, most confusing of all, why was the ball in her hands moving?

Kirsten blinked her eyes open – and groaned. There was a round, firm shape in her hands all right. Unfortunately, it wasn't a football! Footballs didn't have ginger hair.

And they definitely didn't shout "Penalty, Ref!" at the tops of their voices.

In her headlong dive she hadn't grabbed the ball. She'd swooped and grabbed Ginger's head!

"Penalty!" The referee had hared up and was pointing to the spot.

All around her, Kirsten heard the wails of agony from the Angels players.

"A penalty?" cried Tarlock Bhasin. "That's it, then!"

"They can't miss," moaned Lulu Squibb.

"It must be a goal," groaned Jeremy Emery.

All the other Angels players simply sighed hopelessly. Trudging back into her goal, Kirsten knew why. It was because never, ever, in her goalkeeping career had she saved a penalty kick. She'd never even got near to saving one. For some reason, she always guessed the wrong way to dive.

Planting her feet firmly on her goal-line Kirsten crouched, like a determined question mark. In front of her, Ginger had miraculously recovered and was plonking the ball down on the penalty spot. He was going to take the kick himself.

"Get your weight on your left foot," said a quiet voice from behind Kirsten's goal. "That's the way he'll put it. To your left."

To her left! Kirsten flicked an angry glance in Cap Man's direction. What did he know? He didn't look as if he could stop a bottle with a cork!

She turned back to face Ginger. To my right, decided Kirsten, I'll go to my right. Ginger's right-footed, so that's where he'll put the kick. To put it the other way would mean him having to side-foot the ball. In this mud – he won't chance it. To her left, indeed!

Shifting her weight firmly onto her right foot, Kirsten got ready to spring. She was already leaning well to her right as Ginger ran in. The moment he struck the ball, she dived headlong – only to see the ball trickle gently into the opposite corner of the goal.

Cap Man had been right. And she'd guessed wrong again.

❀   ❀   ❀

"Bad luck, Kirsten," said Lennie Gould, the Angels captain, as they trudged back into the changing rooms. "Anyone can make a mistake."

"Yeah," nodded Jonjo Rix seriously. "Easily done. Okay, so heads do have things like ears and noses and eyes and mouths…"

"And ginger hair," chipped in Rhoda O'Neill.

"Right. But apart from that lot – man, a head looks just like a football!"

"Not!" yelled everybody else in unison.

"OK, OK." It was Trevor Rowe, the Angels coach. A hush fell over the room. When Trev spoke, everybody listened. "Look on the bright side. A draw means we're still in the cup. We'll just have to win next Saturday's replay."

"What if it's a draw again?" asked 'Colly' Flower, the team's striker.

"Then there'll be a penalty shoot-out to decide the winners," said Trev.

Everybody looked Kirsten's way. Her heart sank. A penalty shoot-out! If it came to that, the Angels would have no chance.

Unless, that is, she could come up with a plan.

A powerful, penalty-saving plan...

2

Practice Makes...Perfectly Awful!

Practice, that was what Kirsten decided
she needed after some serious thought:
penalty-saving practice, and lots of it.
The others would help her, surely.

She picked up the telephone next morning.
She would start at the top, with Lennie Gould,
the team's captain and chief penalty-taker.

"Lennie, it's Kirsten. How about
getting down to Youth Club an hour early
tonight and giving me some penalty-saving
practice?"

All the Angels players were members of St Jude's Youth Club. The hall they used was next door to St Jude's Church, and there was a perfect strip of grass which ran between the two buildings.

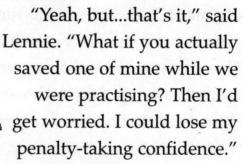

"Er ... I'm not sure." Lennie sounded doubtful.

"Lennie, I need the practice!" Kirsten shouted into the telephone. "I've got to get better at saving penalties!"

"Yeah, but...that's it," said Lennie. "What if you actually saved one of mine while we were practising? Then I'd get worried. I could lose my penalty-taking confidence."

"You wouldn't."

"I would. No, it's too risky. I'm going to spend the week practising against a wall. Sorry."

Kirsten rang Colin Flower, the team's ace striker. He made the same excuse. So did Daisy Higgins when Kirsten rang her. And Jonjo Rix. And Mick Ryall. And the rest of the team. None of the Angels players wanted to take the chance of having their confidence destroyed through Kirsten saving one of their penalty kicks.

"Lionel," sighed Kirsten, dialling one last number. "It'll just have to be Lionel."

Lionel Murgatroyd was Angels' regular substitute, for the simple reason that his ability didn't match his enthusiasm. The only chance Lionel had of getting in the team would be for somebody to break their leg between now and the game.

"Well…all right," said Lionel when Kirsten got through to him. "But I'm not very good, you know that."

⚽   ⚽   ⚽

Youth Club began at 6.30 pm. It was just before 5.30 that Kirsten arrived. Lionel was already waiting, his football boots slung over his shoulder. Together they pushed through the door – only to meet Trev.

"You two are early," he smiled. "The clocks didn't go forward last night, y'know."

Kirsten explained. "This is dedication to duty, Trev. I don't want to make any more gruesome goalkeeping errors on Saturday, so good old Lionel's going to give me an hour's penalty practice on the grass outside."

Trev shook his head. "No he isn't, Kirsten. Not in this weather. Your parents expect me to send you home from Youth Club looking pretty much the same way you arrived – which isn't going to be the case if you spend an hour playing out there."

"Trev!" protested Kirsten. "It's stopped raining! Well, nearly."

"N. O. No!" said Trev. "Look, I've got some work to do before the others turn up. Settle down in the meetings room, eh? If you're lucky you'll find some tasty left-overs in there. One of the parishioners used it for a children's party yesterday."

Glumly, Kirsten led the way to the meetings room. This was a small, comfortable room next to the main hall they used for the Youth Club. It was set out just like a living-room with comfy armchairs, a sideboard, coffee tables, a standard lamp, balloons...

Balloons? Kirsten stopped as she opened the meetings-room door. Of course, the children's party. On the sideboard there was still a large jug of orange juice and various crispy morsels in dishes.

But it was the balloons that gave Kirsten the idea. "Lionel," she said, "I reckon it's practice time!"

"Uh?" said Lionel. "I thought Trev said no playing outside."

"He did. But he didn't say we couldn't play inside, did he? We can practise in here!"

"In here?" Lionel gazed around the room. "What if we smash something? Footballs are hard, y'know."

"But balloons aren't, are they?" Kirsten snatched up the balloon she'd spotted.

"We can't break anything with a balloon! And it'll dip and curve in the air, so it'll be an even better test for my reflexes."

Quickly Kirsten opened the curtains at the end of the room. "The curtains are the goalposts," she said.

She then shoved the armchairs and coffee table to one side, clearing a space in the middle of the room. "One penalty area," she said. Finally, she spread a row of cushions on the floor to dive on. "And one goal-line! Come on, Lionel, penalty time!"

"Are you sure about this?"

"Of course I'm sure," said Kirsten. Pacing as far as she could from her cushion goal-line, she plonked the balloon on a flowery blob of carpet. "That's the penalty spot. It's not the right distance, but it doesn't matter. Balloons don't fly as far as footballs because they're all soft and squashy. That's why there's nothing to worry about, Lionel."

"OK," said Lionel. "Get ready."

Taking a step backwards, Lionel ran in uncertainly. He was never too sure where a football would go when he kicked it, and he was even less sure about a balloon.

As it happened, he struck it well. The balloon shot off towards the left-hand side of the curtains.

Kirsten, true to form, went the wrong way.

Even as she did so, and the balloon slapped against the window for a 'goal', another bright idea whizzed into Kirsten's mind. If her diabolical guessing meant she'd always go the wrong way, perhaps the answer was to practice mid-air changes of direction. And what better time than now?

As the balloon sank to the floor, Kirsten did just that. Twisting in the air, she turned back and leapt on top of it.

Bang!

It was the unexpected suddenness of the sound that did it, coming just as Lionel was breathing a sigh of relief that he'd managed to kick the balloon straight and not hit anything. Startled, he threw up an arm and knocked over the standard lamp.

The lamp toppled over. Its shade flew off and slid the length of the sideboard before clattering into the jug of left-over orange juice. The jug took off. The orange juice cascaded out. And Kirsten, still on the floor directly beneath it, got drowned.

"You couldn't have got much damper if I had let you play outside," said Trev from the doorway.

☸　　　　☸　　　　☸

"I only want to get better at facing penalties," said Kirsten. She was sitting beside the radiator in Trev's study. No longer damp, she was now extremely sticky. "I was thinking of the team."

"I don't know that having you wreck the Youth Club is a price worth paying," said Trev.

"How do I get better then? Got any suggestions?"

Trev looked thoughtful. "Possibly…"

Kirsten leapt to her feet. "What? I'll try anything!"

"Anything?"

"Yes! Yes! Anything at all!"

Trev picked up the phone. "Right. I know that Des Young, one of our parishioners, needs someone to do a little bit of work for him. If you're game, I think I could talk him into giving you some goalkeeping lessons in return."

"Really!" squealed Kirsten. "Is he a goalie, then?"

"Was," said Trev. "A good one, too."

"Ring him up then, Trev. Tell him he's got some help. Kirsten the Kat is on the way!"

3

This Little Piggy...

Wednesday after school found Kirsten
hurrying excitedly away from the main
road and up towards the top of the hill
which was just visible from St Jude's. It
had been a rush to get home and changed
out of her school uniform, but she'd
managed it.

"Old clothes," Trev had said after sorting
out the arrangements with this Des Young
person. "Wear something that can get
dirty – but not your football kit."

Kirsten shrugged. Odd, but who was she to argue? She'd wear a clown's outfit complete with red nose if she ended up a better goalkeeper!

She found the cottage she was looking for halfway up the hill. It was small and square, with a large patch of land at the side. Kirsten ran up and rattled at the door.

Des Young, goalkeeper. What would he look like? she wondered. Tall and wide, probably, with a face that said: "put one past me if you dare!"

The cottage door swung open – and so did Kirsten's mouth. The man in front of her was tall all right. He was quite wide too. What she hadn't expected was that he'd

also be wearing a cap and be holding a
walking-stick. It was Cap Man!

Kirsten was still struggling to overcome
her surprise, even after Des Young had said
hello and started to explain what he wanted
her to do.

"I've got five little 'uns I need some help
with. Their mum's not too well, and so I've
got to give 'em their meals myself."

Five little 'uns? Meals? Surely he doesn't
want me to do the cooking while his wife's
in bed! thought Kirsten.

Des Young hadn't finished, though.

"Trouble is, I'm not too quick on my feet any more," he said, patting his leg. "So I have a bit of trouble rounding them up. That's where you come in, Kirsten. You catch the little rascals for me, and I'll feed 'em."

Rounding up his five children? Was that all? A couple of quick shouts and it would be done. "Fine," said Kirsten. "What are their names?"

"Annie, Wilbur, Buzz, Ruby and Nipper. Nipper's the troublesome one."

"Indoors, are they?"

Des Young frowned and shook his head. "No. They're round the back. Come on, I'll show you."

Kirsten followed him round behind the cottage to where, she was surprised to discover, there was quite a bit more land on which various crops were growing. A section near the cottage had been fenced off, though. Des Young clicked open a gate

leading into this yard and led the way
across to a square brick shed.

"There you go," he said as they reached it,
"all five of 'em are in there."

"In there?" Kirsten could hardly believe
her eyes. The shed was filthy – and it didn't
smell too good, either. "You let your
children play in there!"

"My children?" Des Young smiled, then
broke into a loud laugh. "Kirsten," he said
as reached down and took hold of the
shed's wooden door, "I think there's been

some misunderstanding. Meet Annie, Wilbur, Buzz, Ruby and Nipper!"

He slid the door back. Immediately, what looked like five different-coloured blurs with curly tails shot out and began racing around like mad.

"Piglets!" cried Kirsten.

"Right," said Des Young. "You catch 'em, and then I'll feed 'em from a bottle."

"What about the goalkeeper training?"

"Not until they've all been caught and fed. Especially that one. That's Nipper."

Four of the blurs had stopped running and were now sniffing around but the fifth, the one Des Young was pointing at, was still on the move. Careering around the yard like a bundle of brown and white lightning, it was all Kirsten could do to keep an eye on it.

"No problem," she said. "I'll leave him till last. Let him tire himself out."

"Fine. I'll be indoors. Every time you catch one, bring it over." Des Young walked stiffly back towards the cottage. He stopped at the fence. "Oh, yes. Whatever you do, don't forget to shut this gate.

Leave it open and Nipper will go for it like a bullet. He'll be down to that main road before you know it and that'll be that. Bacon for tea."

As he disappeared into the cottage, Kirsten looked around the yard. This was going to be easy. She'd be practising penalty saves in no time at all. It wasn't that easy, though. Her early attempts at piglet-catching left her empty-handed as Annie accelerated or Buzz buzzed or Wilbur wiggled or Ruby raced away.

Gradually, though, Kirsten got the idea. Waiting until they found some interesting morsel on the ground, she'd tiptoe up behind them and grab them quickly.

"Only Nipper to go now," she said confidently as she brought Ruby in for Des Young to place on his knee and feed with a baby's bottle of milk. "Back in a minute."

In the yard, Nipper had finally stopped running around. Kirsten crept towards him. Nipper gazed up at her, looking as if he was grinning from ear to ear.

Easy, she thought. He's as tired as a full-back who's just spent ninety minutes facing Wayne Rooney. Closer and closer she crept until she was just a few metres away.

That was when Nipper took off, racing straight towards her. Kirsten moved into position to stop him. Too late. Before she'd even bent her knees the piglet had changed direction and shot past her like a bullet.

Kirsten turned to face him again. He was laughing from ear to ear, she was sure he was! Right. This was going to be it. Crouching low, she shuffled slowly fowards in Nipper's direction. Again he took off, straight towards her.

The dumb animal will do the same as last time, reckoned Kirsten. This time, as the piglet drew near, she launched herself into a dive, only to land in something very smelly as Nipper shot by on the other side.

Little had changed an hour later. As Des Young strolled out from the cottage, Nipper was still on the loose.

"Having trouble?"

"Yes, I am!" snapped Kirsten who was by this time feeling very hot and even smellier.

Des Young eased open the gate. "Here, let me show you how."

You are joking! Kirsten thought. If I can't catch him, what chance have you got? She stood back and watched.

Just as she had, Des Young crept closer to Nipper, crouching as he moved. But then, instead of getting nearer, he stopped still. Except that he wasn't totally still, Kirsten could see. He was balancing lightly on his toes.

Suddenly, Nipper did his party trick. Bursting forward, he ran straight towards

Des Young. But the tall man didn't dive. Keeping his eyes fixed firmly on the rocketing piglet, he waited to see which way Nipper was going to go. Then he dived, clutching the squealing piglet in his huge hands.

"Very good," said Kirsten irritably. She followed Des Young as he carried Nipper into the cottage's small kitchen.

"So, goalie training next is it?" she asked as he settled the piglet on his knee.

Des Young looked at his watch. "It would have been if you'd caught Nipper quickly. It's got a bit too late now."

Too late? Kirsten felt as if steam was coming out of her ears. "It wouldn't be too late if you'd come out and caught him an hour ago!" she yelled.

"Look, can you come back Saturday morning? Before your match?"

"And go out on the pitch smelling all horrible? My defenders would conk out!"

"No pig-catching. I promise."

But Kirsten wasn't in a mood to calm down. She'd come here for goalkeeper-training and all she'd been given was the run-around by five little pigs.

"I bet you don't know anything about goalkeeping! I bet you don't know the difference between a penalty spot and a spot on the end of your nose!"

Calmly, Des Young reached to open a cabinet drawer. He took out a small, flat box and handed it to Kirsten.

"Have a look at that when you get home," he said. "Maybe that'll give you more faith in me. You can bring it back with you on Saturday morning."

"If I come!" yelled Kirsten, slamming the door as she marched out.

4

Give her a Medal!

By the time she got home, Kirsten had cooled down a bit. She was also wondering what Des Young had given her to look at.

Sitting on her bed, she opened the box. Inside, lying on a cushion of velvet, was a medal. Kirsten looked – and looked again.

"It's an FA Cup-Winner's medal," she gasped. Turning it over, she looked at the date on the back. Then, rushing for her well-thumbed football encyclopaedia containing every fact a football fanatic could wish to know, she riffled through the pages.

There it was, for the year stamped on the medal. The Cup-winning team. Goalkeeper: D. Young. It was just incredible. She, Kirsten Browne, had met a man who'd climbed the steps to the Royal Box at Wembley.

The next moment she groaned loudly. What had she told him? That she didn't think he knew anything about goalkeeping! That on Saturday morning she might, just might, turn up to be trained by him!

Might? Nothing could stop her going back there now!

It had seemed like the longest week ever. Time and again Kirsten had gazed at Des Young's medal and wondered if Saturday would ever come.

112

She was still looking at it as she reached the bottom of the hill leading up to his cottage, which was why she didn't notice the two boys until they cycled up on either side of her.

"Hey, Brett! Look who it isn't! An Angel. Where's your wings, Angel?"

"She must have lost 'em, Ginger. That's why she always flies the wrong way!"

Kirsten whirled round. It was Ginger, the Harnett team's star. The other boy, Brett Thompson, Kirsten recognised as their substitute.

"So, what's this, Angel?"

Before Kirsten knew it, Ginger had snatched the medal from her hand.

"Give it back."

"Wow! A Cup-winner's medal. Where'd you get it?"

"From a man named Des Young. He was a top goalie. I'm taking it back to him now. He's going to give me some coaching..."

Kirsten knew she'd made a mistake the moment she said it. Tossing the medal to his mate, Ginger yelled, "Go, Brett!"

As his pal raced off, Ginger grinned at Kirsten. "You can have it back after the game, Angel. On one condition."

"What condition?"

"Simple," said Ginger. "Do the same as last week and give us a penalty."

"On purpose?" cried Kirsten.

"You've got it," said Ginger. "Brett will be on the touchline with that medal. When I bang in the penalty, you'll get it back. Right?"

"And if I say no?"

"No penalty, no medal," laughed Ginger, riding off. "See you at the game!"

Kirsten watched him go. What could she do? Without doing what Ginger wanted, she wouldn't get Des Young's medal back. And without that medal she couldn't – she just couldn't – turn up to see him this morning.

She'd just turned round to begin walking home when she heard a shout.

"Kirsten! Stop him!"

Kirsten swung round. The shout had come from Des Young. He was at the far end of the lane. And racing towards her, his little legs whizzing round like Catherine wheels, was Nipper.

"Oh, no! He must have left the gate open!"

If he got past her, Nipper would be at the main road. She had to stop him! Desperately, she tried to remember how Des had done it.

Balanced lightly on his toes for a start, something she'd never done. Kirsten lifted her heels and immediately felt the difference it made. Then, as Nipper came rocketing towards her, she crouched low and kept her eyes fixed on him, just as Des Young had done.

Closer and closer he got. Still Kirsten didn't move. Only when she saw Nipper dart to one side did she take a flying leap. Both her hands closed over the little pink body. Nipper squealed and wriggled. She'd caught him! Des Young came hurrying down the lane towards her. "Brilliant, Kirsten. I'm glad you turned up after all." "Er…" stammered Kirsten. What could she do now? She couldn't possibly tell him about the medal.

"I…I only came to say I couldn't come, if you know what I mean. And…I've forgotten your medal, I'm afraid. I'll bring it back after the match."

Handing over the wriggling Nipper before Des Young could say a word, Kirsten raced off.

If she was going to get his medal back, she had some serious thinking to do before the match began.

5

Remember Nipper!

Ginger and Brett sidled up to her as the teams filed out onto the pitch.

"Remember, Angel," whispered Ginger, threateningly. "No penalty…"

"No medal…" said Brett the substitute, patting the pocket of his tracksuit top.

"What did Ginger want?" asked Bazza Watts as the two Harnett players sprinted off. "Asking you to leave his head alone this time, was he?"

"Asking her to grab it, more like," said Daisy. "He scored from the penalty, remember."

Jonjo Rix looked at Kirsten. "Repeat after me: footballs do not have ginger hair, footballs do not have ginger hair..."

"All right," said Kirsten. "If you bang in a dozen goals it won't matter, will it?"

But, as she took her place in goal, she knew that wasn't likely. Like the first match, this one was going to be a tight game. A penalty could make all the difference.

So it proved. The two teams were evenly matched and the first half ended without either team having had any real scoring chances.

"I can see this ending in a penalty shoot-out," said Colly Flower glumly.

"Me too," said Rhoda O'Neill.

Kirsten knew what they were thinking, because she was thinking the same. Balloon practice, pig practice – her plans had ended in disaster. On top of that, there was Des Young's medal and Ginger's threat. She knew what she had to do. The question was: how?

The second half began. A quick Harnett raid was ended by Kirsten whipping the ball off the end of Ginger's toe. "No penalty…" he murmured as he ran back.

Kirsten pretended not to hear. She threw the ball out to Tarlock Bhasin. Playing a quick one-two with Daisy Higgins, Tarlock took the ball as far as the half-way line before releasing it to Colly Flower. As Colly looked around, apparently unsure who to pass to, Tarlock kept going.

It was a great tactic. Colly switched direction and hammered the ball to the unmarked Tarlock who raced on down to the byline before pulling the ball back for Jonjo Rix to bang into the roof of the net. 1-0 to the Angels!

Everybody except Kirsten jumped for joy. All she could think about was Des Young's medal and how she was going to get it back.

The game restarted, but the Angels were playing really well. So many Harnett attacks were being broken down that Kirsten was almost a spectator. With only a few minutes left, she'd had no chance to do what she planned to do.

Out on the touchline, Harnett were preparing to bring on their substitute in a last-gasp effort to save the game. Brett Thompson was running down the touchline to warm up.

Suddenly, Harnett broke away, Ginger racing on to a long ball over Bazza Watts' head. It was the chance Kirsten had been waiting for. As Bazza turned to give chase, Kirsten raced from her goal.

"Penalty, Angel!" yelled Ginger as, with Bazza right behind him, he hared into the penalty box.

But Kirsten had her plan, and it didn't include doing what he wanted. Reaching the ball first, she hammered it hard and low off the pitch – straight into Brett Thompson's stomach! As he collapsed in a heap, and Ginger did the same thing behind her, Kirsten raced off the pitch.

"Poor Brett," she cried, bending down, "are you all right?"

"Shove...off!" gasped the substitute. "You did that...on purpose!"

"Too right," said Kirsten, whipping the FA Cup medal out of his pocket. "It worked, as well!"

"Do you want me to take that?"

As she turned to see Des Young, Kirsten nodded dumbly. He must have been watching all the time.

"Thanks," he said as Kirsten handed it over. "Now, you go and save that penalty."

"Penalty? What penalty?"

"Your full-back reached that ginger-headed lad just as you whacked the ball into touch. Didn't touch him, but he leapt into the air as if he'd been kicked by an elephant. Fooled the referee, too. He's given a penalty."

Kirsten turned back to the match. Ginger was busy putting the ball on the spot.

"If only I'd got that coaching from you," she wailed.

Des Young grinned. "But you did," he said. "How did you catch Nipper? Stayed on your toes, kept your eyes on him and moved when you saw which way he was going. If that's not goalkeeping I don't know what is! Go on, get in that goal and do the same!"

Kirsten went back to stand on her goal-line.

She bounced on her toes, instead of standing flat-footed.

As Ginger ran in, she didn't look at him. Instead, just as she had with Nipper, she kept her eyes glued to the ball until she saw which way it was going.

Only then did Kirsten leap that way – the right way – to snaffle the ball with both hands! She'd saved it!

"Well done," said Des Young as the Angels ran out 1-0 winners.

Kirsten beamed. "Thanks to you. I wish you'd told me Nipper-chasing was goal-keeper training. I wouldn't have got so annoyed."

"Sorry about that. I was going to tell you on Saturday morning, but you rushed off too quickly."

"I didn't want to tell you about your medal."

"I wouldn't have minded," said Des Young.

"Wouldn't have minded!" cried Kirsten. "I imagined you'd go bananas! If I won a Cup Final medal I wouldn't let it out of my sight!"

The ex-goalkeeper grinned. "Me neither." He pulled the medal he'd loaned to Kirsten from his pocket. "That's why I had this copy made. The real one's at home, safe and sound!"

DIRTY
DEFENDING

CONTENTS

1

Trev Branches Out

"Who are the best?" bawled Lennie Gould.

"Angels! Angels!" hollered the other members of the Angels FC team.

"Who'll smash the rest?"

"Angels! Angels!"

The team minibus was still echoing as it came to a halt with a squeak. The driver turned to look at Lennie.

"An interesting song, Lennie," said Trevor Rowe, the Angels manager. "Of course, when you say 'smash', I know you mean 'beat with pure football skill', not…"

"Smash 'em to pulp?" said Lennie innocently. "'Course not, Trev!"

"I'm pleased to hear it," said Trev. "Because you know the Angels code…"

Everybody knew what was coming next. The team weren't called the Angels for nothing. They represented St Jude's Youth Club – and as the vicar of St Jude's Church as well as their team manager, Trev was very keen on fair play. So before he could finish, the whole team chanted…

ANGELS ON AND OFF THE PITCH!

Trev smiled. "Correct. No dirty defending or terrible tackling."

"Not even against Rockley Demons?" shouted Kirsten Browne, the Angels goalkeeper.

"Especially against Rockley Demons," said Trev, sliding open the minibus doors. "Let's beat them fair and square."

"Let's beat 'em up," muttered Lennie to Kirsten as they clambered out of the bus.

The Angels were competing in the annual Clackett Football Festival. There were three other teams against them, including the previous year's winners, Rockley Demons.

Lennie's top lip curled. "Remember their captain, 'Hacker' Haynes? I've got a score to settle with him—"

He was interrupted by a high-pitched squeal. "Leonard!! Oh, Leonard! Let me look at you!"

Lennie looked up in panic. Hurrying towards him was a woman with hair like a fluffy blancmange. Before he could move, she'd grabbed him.

"Leonard! Haven't you grown!"

"Hello, Aunt Grace," mumbled Lennie.

His Aunt Grace. The tidiest person in Tidy City.

Lennie felt his hair being smoothed flat. "Lost your comb again, though!" The blancmange looked down. "And forgotten to polish your shoes!"

"They're trainers, Aunt Grace," said Lennie. "You don't polish trainers."

It was Trev who came to Lennie's rescue. "Hello, Mrs Gould. Thank you so much for letting us camp out with you."

Lennie's Aunt Grace had recently moved to Clackett and she'd written to Trev offering to let the Angels camp in her gigantic garden, rather than jam into Clackett's Field with the other teams.

"Where do you want us to pitch our tents?" asked Trev.

"Why don't you go to the bottom of the garden, near the trees?" said Aunt Grace, pointing. Far in the distance, Lennie could just make out the trees she was talking about. "You won't be disturbed down there – except by Clackett's Ghost!"

"Clackett's Ghost?" said Bazza Watts, the Angels right-back.

"Clackett's Headless Ghost," said Aunt Grace, her eyes opening wide. "Apparently the original Farmer Clackett had a nasty accident with a very sharp scythe. It's said that his ghost walks at midnight with his head under his arm, looking for somebody who can fix it back on again—"

"Talking of fixing," interrupted Trev quickly, "it's time we fixed our tents. If we're quick we can get in a training session before supper."

139

The Angels team were gathered at the far end of Aunt Grace's garden, beneath two trees they'd been using as goalposts.

"I've been thinking about corner kicks," said Trev.

Lennie felt a spurt of excitement. When Trev said he'd been thinking, it meant he'd got something good up his sleeve.

"Instead of just heaving our corners into a crowded penalty area," Trev went on, "why don't we try something different? I call it Plan 34B, and it goes something like this…" He explained his idea slowly.

"OK?" Everybody nodded. "Right. Defenders, to your positions. Attackers to yours. And wait till I say go," he called.

"What are you doing?" called Lennie, as Trev began to climb one of their goalpost trees.

"Getting a grandstand view," puffed Trev as he made his way up. "From here I'll be able to see if you're all running to the right places." He hauled himself on to a branch jutting out like a high crossbar. "Perfect!" he cried. "Right, plan 34B – go!"

Immediately, his plan swung into action. Mick Ryall, the team's right winger, ran in as if he was taking a corner kick. At the same time, Jonjo Rix and Colin "Colly" Flower, the Angels striker, began to move. Jonjo went one way, while Colly dashed towards Mick Ryall calling, "Short one, Mick!"

The winger drove the ball towards him. Instead of controlling it, though, Colly simply let it run through his legs.

This was the moment Lennie had been waiting for. With different defenders moving towards both Jonjo and Colly, a gap had opened up beautifully, just as Trev had said it would. Sprinting forward, Lennie ran on to the ball. Wallop! He hit a rocket shot straight for the top corner of Kirsten's goal.

As he watched it go, Lennie was full of admiration for their coach. Trev had thought it out perfectly...almost.

The only thing he hadn't considered was the possibility that Kirsten might actually reach Lennie's shot. And she did. With an almighty leap, her fingers tipped the ball upwards...

"Aaaaaaagggghhhh!"

The ambulance, called by Aunt Grace the moment she'd seen Trev lying on the ground beneath a pile of twigs and leaves, arrived quickly.

The driver got out and crouched over him.

"How many fingers?" he said, holding his hand up.

The Angels manager frowned. "Ten. No, eight. Hang on, twelve. No, that can't be right. Ask me something easier."

"How many heads has he got?" said Lennie.

"Thanks, Lennie. That's more like it." Trev looked hard at the ambulance driver's peaked cap. "Two…"

"Concussion, I reckon," said the man as Trev was laid on a stretcher and trundled towards the waiting ambulance. "They'll probably keep him in for twenty-four hours' observation."

"Twenty-four hours!" exclaimed Lennie. "But they can't! We'll have to scratch from the tournament!"

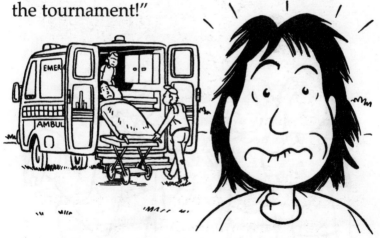

"Scratch, Leonard?" said Aunt Grace. "Whatever for?"

145

"We have to have a manager with us," said Jeremy Emery, one of the Angels centre-backs. "It's in the rules."

Aunt Grace shrugged. "So? I'll be your manager."

"You?" said Lennie.

"Do you know anything about football, Mrs Gould?" asked Kirsten.

"No," said Aunt Grace. "Why? Does it matter?"

At the ambulance doors, Trev weakly
lifted his head from the stretcher.
"Remember the Angels code," he mumbled.
"Angels on and off the pitch. Keep it
clean…"

"There you are," said Aunt Grace, as Trev
was driven off to hospital. She wagged a
finger at them all. "That's all I need to know.
Keep it clean!"

2

Aunt Grace Cleans Up

"Well, well. If it ain't Lennie the Lemon. Back for another dose of Hacker's medicine, are yah?"

The Rockley Demons' captain, Hacker Haynes, had been waiting for Lennie outside the changing rooms.

"Medicine, Hacker? I don't feel sick. Except when I look at you!"

Hacker Haynes's bottom lip curled out like a banana. "We'll see who feels sick tomorrow," he snarled. "When we play you Angels!"

Lennie was just about to do something very unangelic when he heard a loud trill.

"Leonard! Oh, Leonard!"

It was Aunt Grace. She was immaculately dressed, from her shining black shoes to a hat covered in more flowers than most gardens. Over one arm she was carrying an umbrella, and over the other a bulging straw bag.

"Who's this?" asked Hacker Haynes, laughing. "Your manager?"

"Quite correct," trilled Aunt Grace. She looked down her nose at the boy. "Are you one of my Angels?"

"Me?" snorted Hacker. "No chance!"

"Good," retorted Aunt Grace. She turned to Lennie. "Now, Leonard. Do any of you want a pair of gloves? It's quite nippy out here in the open."

"Gloves?" Lennie gurgled.

Aunt Grace opened her straw bag. "Or a scarf? How about a hot-water bottle to tuck inside your vest?"

That was it! Hacker Haynes began to screech with laughter. "Hot-water bottles! What a load of wimps! We're gonna make mincemeat of you lot!" He headed off across Clackett's Field to the pitch Rockley Demons were playing on, still laughing.

Lennie felt his face go red. "Aunt Grace, we're playing football, not trekking to the North Pole!"

"Well, just tell everybody they're in my bag if they want them."

A whistle sounded. On another pitch, the referee was ready to start the Angels game against Weston Sparks.

"I've got to go and toss up, Aunt Grace." Lennie sighed. "Is there anything else?"

"Only one thing," said Aunt Grace sharply. "The most important thing. Remember what Trevor said: 'Angels on and off the pitch. Keep it clean!'"

Relieved to have escaped from Aunt Grace, Lennie threw himself into the match against Weston Sparks.

With only a minute gone, he slithered in to win the ball with a sliding tackle that left a streak of mud all the way down the back of his football shirt. Passing to Bazza Watts, he sprinted forward into the Weston penalty area. Over came Bazza's cross – and Lennie dived full-length to score with a rocketing header!

Running back to the centrespot, the front
of his football shirt now covered in mud too,
Lennie looked over at Aunt Grace. Even
somebody who knew nothing about football
must have been pleased with that goal, he
thought. But for some reason Aunt Grace
looked anything but pleased. She was
jabbing her umbrella angrily into the
ground and looking as if she'd just
swallowed a slug.

The rest of the Angels players, though,
were inspired by Lennie's example.

Slithering and sliding, leaping and diving, they didn't give Weston a chance. Two more goals – a brave header from leftwinger Rhoda O'Neill that left her face down in the mud, and a penalty from striker Colly Flower after he'd been sent sprawling – saw the Angels run out comfortable 3–0 winners.

"The Demons only won 2–1," said Kirsten as they came off the pitch. "That puts us on top on goal difference."

	P	W	D	L	F	A	PTS
Angels FC	1	1	0	0	3	0	3
Rockley Demons	1	1	0	0	2	1	3
Hursley Hornets	1	0	0	1	1	2	0
Weston Sparks	1	0	0	1	0	3	0

"So why doesn't our acting manager look pleased, Lennie?" said Daisy Higgins, rubbing a pair of muddy hands on the remaining patch of white on her shorts.

Aunt Grace was stalking towards them, still with her slug-swallowing look.

"Maybe she thinks we should have scored more goals," said Lennie.

But Aunt Grace said nothing about goals. "Get changed at once," she snapped.

Lennie frowned. "Get changed? It's hardly worth it. We're playing our second game straight after lunch."

"At once!" screeched Aunt Grace. She shook her head. "Oh, Leonard. I am very disappointed in you!"

"Keep it clean," said Aunt Grace seriously. "They were Trevor's express instructions. And what happens? You all come off the field looking like mud pies!"

They were eating their lunch in Aunt Grace's spotless kitchen. Around the walls, every pot and pan was in its place and shining brightly.

"Aunt Grace," said Lennie, "Trev didn't mean we couldn't get ourselves dirty. He meant no dirty play. No fouling."

But Aunt Grace was having none of it. "Leonard, really! If that was what he meant, he would have said so. But he said 'Keep it clean.'"

"That's right!" pleaded Lennie. "Angels on and off the pitch!"

"Pre-cisely!" said Aunt Grace. "And what colour do angels wear? White! Spotless white!"

"But—"

"Enough!" snapped Aunt Grace. "You will stay clean for this afternoon's game. And if you do not…I will withdraw you from the competition!"

"Now what do we do?" said Lulu Squibb, the Angels tough-tackling midfield player, as Aunt Grace stalked from the kitchen.

Lennie thought for a moment. "No problem," he said finally. "After this morning's game our kit couldn't get any dirtier!"

"Wrong, Leonard." It was Aunt Grace, back again with a bundle of washing in her arms. "Your football kit," she announced, "clean again. And it had better stay that way. Or else!"

"She can't be serious!" said Bazza Watts as the Angels gathered together before their afternoon match against Hursley Hornets.

"She looked pretty serious to me," said Kirsten, pulling on her freshly washed goalkeeper's gloves.

Lennie looked embarrassed. "I know. We'd better not take any chances. Try to keep clean, everybody!"

It wasn't easy. With just five minutes gone Lennie moved in to break up a Hursley attack. But just as he was about to launch himself into one of his usual sliding tackles, he remembered Aunt Grace's instructions and stopped.

The Hursley player dribbled through but, surprised at not being tackled, pushed it too close to Kirsten in the Angels goal. She charged out, but suddenly stopped and let the ball bounce straight past her before racing back and just managing to kick it off for a corner!

"Why didn't you slide-tackle him?" she shouted.

"To stay clean!" yelled Lennie. "Why didn't you dive on it?"

"Same as you – to stay clean!"

"Oh, this is ridiculous," said Tarlock Bhasin, the left back. "What are we going to do?"

"There's only one thing we can do," said Lennie. "Keep passing the ball to each other. That way Hursley won't get it and we won't get dirty trying to win it back."

And so, for the rest of the most boring 0–0 draw in football history, the Angels passed the ball round and round in circles, staying clean but going nowhere until the referee thankfully blew his whistle for full-time.

"Demons won 6–1!" crowed Hacker Haynes as he passed Lennie on the way to the changing rooms. "That puts us on top. You'll have to beat us to win the title, Lemon – so you've got no chance!"

	P	W	D	L	F	A	PTS
Rockley Demons	2	2	0	0	8	2	6
Angels FC	2	1	1	0	3	0	4
Hursley Hornets	2	0	1	1	1	2	1
Weston Sparks	2	0	0	2	1	9	0

"We can do it," said Lennie to Kirsten. "Trev will be back with us this evening."

"Sorry, dear, he won't." It was Aunt Grace, looking pleased as she came up to check Lennie's sparkling and unmuddy shorts.

"They're keeping him in hospital until tomorrow." She trotted off to examine the other Angels shirts for any specks of mud, calling as she went, "You can't blame them. Trevor still thinks the doctor's head is in the wrong place."

"Keeping him in? That means she'll still be our manager!" wailed Kirsten. "Lennie, what can we do?"

"Head in the wrong place," muttered Lennie. "Did you hear that?"

"What?"

"Head in the wrong place," repeated Lennie. "That's what we can do!" A grin spread across his face. "Kirsten, meet me at midnight."

"At midnight? What on earth for?"

"To see Clackett's Ghost walk again!"

3

Woo-Wooooo!

Lennie slipped from his sleeping bag and crept out of his tent.

Kirsten was already waiting for him. "This had better be good," she whispered and yawned at the same time. "I need my sleep. You don't want me dropping off against a goalpost tomorrow, do you?"

"It'll be good," whispered Lennie. "I've got this all worked out." Stopping only to pick up the plain white practice football they'd been using for a kick-about after supper, Lennie led

Kirsten across to the far side of Aunt Grace's massive garden. There, hidden behind a thatch of dense shrubbery, was a solid wooden shed.

"I spotted this place earlier," said Lennie. "It's just perfect!"

"What for?"

"You'll see."

Lennie undid the catch on the shed door and slipped inside. Moments later, he was out again, this time holding a brush and a tin of black paint.

"Now what are you doing?" mumbled Kirsten, as Lennie began to dab paint on the football.

"Getting ahead!" laughed Lennie as he held up the finished article. The ball now had eyes, a nose and a gaping mouth.

"I'm going to snaffle a sheet from Aunt Grace's washing line, chuck it over my head and hold this ball under my arm."

"But why?" said Kirsten, rubbing her eyes. "And why did you say this shed was perfect?"

Lennie sighed. "Because when I moan my head off outside Aunt Grace's window and she thinks I'm Clackett's Ghost and comes out to investigate and follows me, I'm going to lead her to this shed, right? And all you've got to do…is shut her in!"

"Me?" Kirsten yawned another mighty yawn.

"Yes, you!" hissed Lennie, starting off towards Aunt Grace's cottage. "And Kirsten – don't go to sleep before I get here!"

As Lennie went, Kirsten blinked herself awake. Could it really work? It would be brilliant if it did. With no Aunt Grace to stop them playing their normal game they'd beat Rockley Demons easily. They could let her out of the shed after the Angels had won the title.

Creeping round behind the shed, Kirsten waited in the shadows. She shivered in the deathly quiet – and then jumped as a loud crack sounded from somewhere nearby. She whirled round, but all she could see were more shadows.

Then she heard rustling noises come from another direction. She swung round again, her hair standing on end and an awful, terrible thought in her mind: could it be…could it possibly be…the real Clackett's Ghost?

"Who – who – who's there?" she called.

From behind her came a horrible, horrible laugh! Kirsten opened her mouth to scream, but before she could make a sound, a blanket was thrown over her head! She felt a rope being wound around her. Moments later she was scooped off her feet and carried away…

Again she heard the horrible, horrible laugh – but this time it was accompanied by a horrible, horrible voice: "Let's see Lemon's Angels beat us without their goalie!"

It was the horrible, horrible voice of Hacker Haynes.

⚽   ⚽   ⚽

Lennie crept up to the cottage. Aunt Grace's washing line was swinging gently near the back door, layers of snowy-white sheets hanging from it.

Lennie whipped one off and threw it over his head. Then, tucking the ghost-head football under his arm, he shuffled round to a spot beneath his aunt's bedroom window.

"Woo-wooo!" he began to wail. "Woo-wooo!"

Up above, the room stayed in darkness.

Lennie tried again, louder this time: "Woo-wooooo!"

A light flicked on. She was getting up! Lennie threw in an extra big moan: "Woooo-wooooooooooo!"

The curtains swung open – and Lennie nearly jumped in fright himself as Aunt Grace's head, swathed in curlers, appeared at the window. Slowly, he backed away. Up at the window, Aunt Grace stared for a moment until, suddenly, she disappeared from view.

170

She was coming after him!

Seconds later the cottage door opened. Out came Aunt Grace, her nightdress billowing and her umbrella waving above her head. "Come back!" she cried.

Lennie was going to do nothing of the sort. Racing across the garden, he headed for the shed. The door was still wide open, as he'd left it. But where was Kirsten? She must be hiding somewhere, Lennie decided. Dropping the football and throwing off his sheet, he dived into the bushes.

"Get ready, Kirsten!" he hissed. "She's coming!"

Aunt Grace hurried up. Seeing the open shed door, she stopped. "Are you in there?" Lennie heard her say.

He leaned out for a better view. His aunt was slowly inching her way towards the shed. Where was Kirsten? He watched Aunt Grace tiptoe right up to the shed door, her umbrella held out in front of her like a sword. Still no Kirsten. Where was she?

As his aunt stepped into the shed, Lennie realised there was only one thing for it. Leaping from his hiding place he shot across the grass like a rocket and slammed the shed door shut. Moments later the catch was in place and he'd jammed a garden roller against the door for good measure. Aunt Grace was well and truly trapped.

"I don't know," muttered Lennie, ignoring the muffled shouts coming from the shed as he looked around for Kirsten.

"If you want a job done properly, you've got to do it yourself. I bet the dozy article's gone back to bed." He began the long trek back to his tent. "Just wait till I see her in the morning…"

4

Lemme Out!

"Do you know where she is, Lennie?" asked Jeremy Emery anxiously as he, Lennie and Colly walked towards the changing rooms the next morning.

Lennie grinned. "Let's just say she won't be coming, Jez. Because she…ha-ha…she couldn't get away!"

A look of horror crossed Jeremy's face. "What? She won't be coming! That's a disaster! We'll be lost without her!"

"What are you on about?" said Lennie.

"She's the last person we want around, isn't she?"

Jeremy looked at him. "How can you say that about her?"

"About my Aunt Grace? I thought everybody was saying that about her!"

Colly looked blank. "Her? We're not talking about Batty-woman. We're talking about Kirsten!"

"Kirsten? Why, where is she?"

Colly jumped up and down in agony. "That's why we asked if you knew where she was! Nobody's seen her this morning!"

Daisy Higgins, Lulu Squibb and Rhoda O'Neill came hurrying up. "There's no sign of her," said Daisy. "We've looked everywhere!"

"What's the matter? Lost sumfink?" It was Hacker Haynes, surrounded by his Demons team-mates. "Or somebody?"

"Kirsten," said Lennie. "Do you know where she is?"

"Somewhere you won't find her," cackled Hacker. "At least, not until after the Demons have mangled you!"

That must have been why Kirsten disappeared last night, Lennie realised. Hacker must have heard him arranging to meet her and grabbed her while he was haunting Aunt Grace!

He had to do something, tell somebody...

Whoa! He couldn't do that. If he did, he'd also have to explain why they'd been out and about in the middle of the night. His

lock-away-Aunt-Grace plan would be
revealed. He'd be found guilty of
Aunt-napping and locked up himself!

No, there was only one thing he could do.
It would be tricky, but it might work...

"Bazza," yelled Lennie, "start the game
without us. I'm going to find Kirsten!"

"What?" said Bazza. "Who's going
in goal?"

"We haven't got Lionel or Ricky with us,
so you'll have to! I'll be back as soon as I
can. Try to hang on!"

Off he raced, across Clackett's Field,
through the trees surrounding it, over the
high wall at the end of them – and into
Aunt Grace's garden. Right in front of him
was the wooden shed.

If anybody knew where Kirsten could
have been hidden, it would be Aunt Grace.
After all, she lived in Clackett, so she'd
know all the likely spots.

He tiptoed up to the shed door. Then, moving the roller away, Lennie flung the door open. Aunt Grace shot out as if she'd been fired from a cannon. Her face was grimy and she looked ready to do something truly awful with the umbrella in her hand.

Yes, thought Lennie, this was going to be the tricky bit...

"Aunt Grace!" he cried at once. "Thank goodness I've found you! Oh, I've been so worried about you!"

It worked – beautifully. Before he knew it, Aunt Grace was smothering him in kisses.

"Leonard, I've been in that shed all night! Some slimy toad played a trick on me and shut me in!"

"Er…slimy toad?"

"If I ever find out who it was I will strangle them!" roared Aunt Grace.

Lennie didn't dwell on the thought. Enlisting his aunt's help in finding Kirsten was the important thing.

"Kirsten's been shut away somewhere too!"

Aunt Grace looked as if she was about to breathe fire. "I know!" she shouted.

"You do?" said Lennie. "How?"

"Because I've been shut in here all night as well, dimbo!" And out of the shed stepped a bedraggled Kirsten.

Lennie stared open-mouthed.

"Hacker Haynes and his gang shoved me in here just before—"

Lennie stopped her in panic. "Before… before what?"

"Before they locked me in!" screeched Aunt Grace. "I saw one of them pinching my sheet and ran out after him. When I got here I heard Kirsten struggling in the shed. No sooner had I gone in to have a look than—"

"Hacker Haynes shut you in as well!" cried Lennie. "That's what must have happened, Aunt Grace!"

He darted across to where the painted football was still on the ground. "Proof!" he shouted. "Hacker Haynes plays football!"

Aunt Grace's eyes narrowed. When she spoke it was as if her voice was dripping icicles. "Who exactly is this Haynes toad?"

It was all working out brilliantly!

"He's the captain of the team we're playing this morning. We've got to beat them to win the title—" Lennie looked up as the shriek of a whistle came from the direction of Clackett's Field. "And the game's just started!"

"Then get moving, the two of you!" shouted Aunt Grace.

Lennie and Kirsten began sprinting away, only to stop again as Aunt Grace called, "Oh, and Leonard…"

"Yes, Aunt Grace?"

"You remember what Trevor said about keeping it clean?"

"Yes, Aunt Grace." Lennie nodded glumly.

Aunt Grace gave the ghost-head football a vicious thump with her umbrella. "Well, forget it! As far as this Haynes toad is concerned, you can get as disgustingly dirty as you like!"

5

Plan 34B

"At last!" shouted Bazza Watts as Lennie and
Kirsten raced on to the pitch. "We're 1–0
down already."

"What happened?" panted Lennie.

"Goalmouth scramble. Their winger scored
while Hacker Haynes was sitting on me." Bazza
pulled off the goalkeeper's jersey and handed it
to Kirsten. "The ref said he didn't see a thing."

"Course he didn't," snarled Hacker, running
past. "Too smart, ain't I? So watch out, Lemon.
I'm after you."

Everywhere Lennie went Hacker Haynes went too, digging his elbows in Lennie's ribs and kicking at his ankles. By half-time Lennie was covered in bruises but the referee hadn't spoken to Hacker once.

Aunt Grace, now fully dressed, was waiting for them on the touchline. "Is that the Haynes toad?" she asked, pointing with her umbrella.

Lennie nodded. "That's him."

Aunt Grace's eyes narrowed.
"Leonard, be a good boy. When you start playing again, see if you can bring him in my direction."

Lennie couldn't imagine what she had in mind, but as the second half got under way the chance came for him to do just what Aunt Grace wanted. In defence, Tarlock Bhasin won the ball with a good tackle.

"Down the line, Tarlock!' yelled Lennie, racing out to the touchline with Hacker in hot pursuit.

Lennie controlled Tarlock's pass. As he did so, Hacker dived in but Lennie gave him the slip, feinting to cut inside before sprinting on down the wing, to where Aunt Grace was standing on the touchline.

"I'm gonna get you, Lemon!" shouted Hacker, chasing after Lennie. "Hacker's gonna hack…oompph!!"

Aunt Grace had looped the handle of her umbrella round Hacker's ankle and sent him flying nose-first into the mud!

Lennie ran on down the wing. As a Demons defender came to tackle him, he slipped the ball inside for Jonjo Rix to bang into the net. Demons 1, Angels 1!

"No goal, referee!" roared Hacker Haynes from out on the touchline. "He tripped me up!"

The referee shook his head as he ran back to the centre circle. "I didn't see anything."

"It must have been Clackett's Ghost!" cackled Aunt Grace.

An enraged Hacker leapt to his feet. "It was a foul, I tell you!"

"And I'm telling you I didn't see anything," replied the referee.

"Well, you wouldn't, would you!" bawled Hacker without thinking. "I've been fouling all game and you haven't seen one of them either…"

"Oh, you have, have you?" said the referee. "Well, in that case, I'll have my eye on you from now on. One dodgy move and it'll be a red card."

The game restarted. With Hacker worried about being sent off, Lennie had more chance to play. Slowly, the Angels got on top. With just five minutes to go they won a corner out on the right. That was when Lennie heard the call.

Plan 34B!

"Hey, it's Trev!" shouted Lennie. "They must have let him out of hospital. Come on, let's give it a try."

As Mick Ryall ran out to take the corner, Hacker Haynes planted himself in front of Lennie. "You can plan all you like, Lemon," he growled, "but I'm gonna stick to you like chewing gum."

"Suit yourself," said Lennie, and shrugged. He began to amble away from the goal. "Plan 34B doesn't include me."

Hacker frowned.

As Mick Ryall started to take the corner, Hacker frowned a bit more. Finally, as Jonjo started to run one way and Colly dashed out towards the corner flag yelling, "Short one, Mick!" and Lennie still didn't move, Hacker finally decided that plan 34B really didn't involve Lennie.

So he dashed after Colly – only to find the ball whizzing past him as the Angels striker let it run through his legs and on to the unmarked Lennie, who smacked it gleefully into the net for the winning goal!

	P	W	D	L	F	A	PTS
Angels FC	3	2	1	0	5	1	7
Rockley Demons	3	2	0	1	9	4	6
Hursley Hornets	3	0	2	1	3	4	2
Weston Sparks	3	0	1	2	3	11	1

"Well done, team!" said a beaming Trev as the Angels brought the trophy across to show him.

Lennie grinned. "Well done to you too, Trev. Plan 34B worked a treat that time."

"Been a bit of a weekend for plans, hasn't it?" Kirsten grinned at Lennie.

"It has indeed," said Aunt Grace icily. She dipped into her enormous bag and pulled out the football with the ghost-face painted on it. "Now, if you'll excuse me, Trevor, I'm just going to return this ball to its rightful owner."

"Rightful owner?" said Trev.

"A toad named Haynes."

"Mrs Gould, I think there's been some mistake," said Trev. Taking the ball from Aunt Grace, he turned it round to the other side of the painted face and pointed to a stamp mark. "'Property of Angels FC'. This is one of our footballs."

Aunt Grace looked at the mark. She looked at Trev. Finally, she looked at the boy trying to hide behind the trophy his team had just won.

"Leonard..." she growled.